Bumpus Jumpus Dinosaurumpus

For Maud, Milly and Ben – T.M.

For Sarah, with love – G.P-R.

ORCHARD BOOKS

First published in Great Britain in 2002 by The Watts Publishing Group

This edition first published in 2016

Text © Tony Mitton 2002

Illustrations © Guy Parker Rees 2002

The moral rights of the author and illustrator have been asserted.

All rights reserved.

A CIP catalogue record for this book is available from the British Library.

ISBN 978 1 40835 034 8

Printed and bound in China

Orchard Books

An imprint of Hachette Children's Group

Part of The Watts Publishing Group Limited

Carmelite House

50 Victoria Embankment

London EC4Y 0DZ

An Hachette UK Company

www.hachette.co.uk

www.hachettechildrens.co.uk

Bumpus Jumpus Dinosaurumpus

Tony Mitton

Guy Parker-Rees

ORCHARD

There's a quake and a quiver
and a rumbling around.

It makes you shiver.
It's a thundery sound.

"Shake, shake, shudder...
near the sludgy old swamp.
The dinosaurs are coming.
Get ready to romp.

Donk!

Donk!

Donk!

Here's **Triceratops** jumping UP and DOWN doing dinosaur hops.

He wears three horns
on his **big**, bony head,

and blunders along with a
Bomp! Bomp! tread.

"Shake, shake, shudder"...
near the sludgy old swamp.
The dinosaurs are coming.
Get ready to romp.

Watch out for
Deinosuchus
with her
snip-snap grin,
as she perches
on her tail and
twizzles
in a spin.

BrontoSaurus stops
for a slushy, mushy snack.
His tail starts swinging with a

Thwack! Thwack! Thwack!
"Shake, shake, shudder"...
near the sludgy old swamp.
The dinosaurs are coming.
Get ready to romp.

Stegosaurus stomps along
with lots of her mates.

Clatter! **Clatter!** **Clatter!**

go their bony
back plates.

"Shake, shake, shudder"...
near the sludgy old swamp.
The dinosaurs are coming.
Get ready to romp.

Styracosaurus shakes
his collar and his spikes.
Rattle! Rattle! Rattle!
is the noise that he likes!

A pack of **Deinonychuses**
go running by fast
with a Zoom! Zoom! Zoom!
so they won't be the last.

"Shake, shake, shudder"...
near the sludgy old swamp.
The dinosaurs are coming.
Get ready to romp.

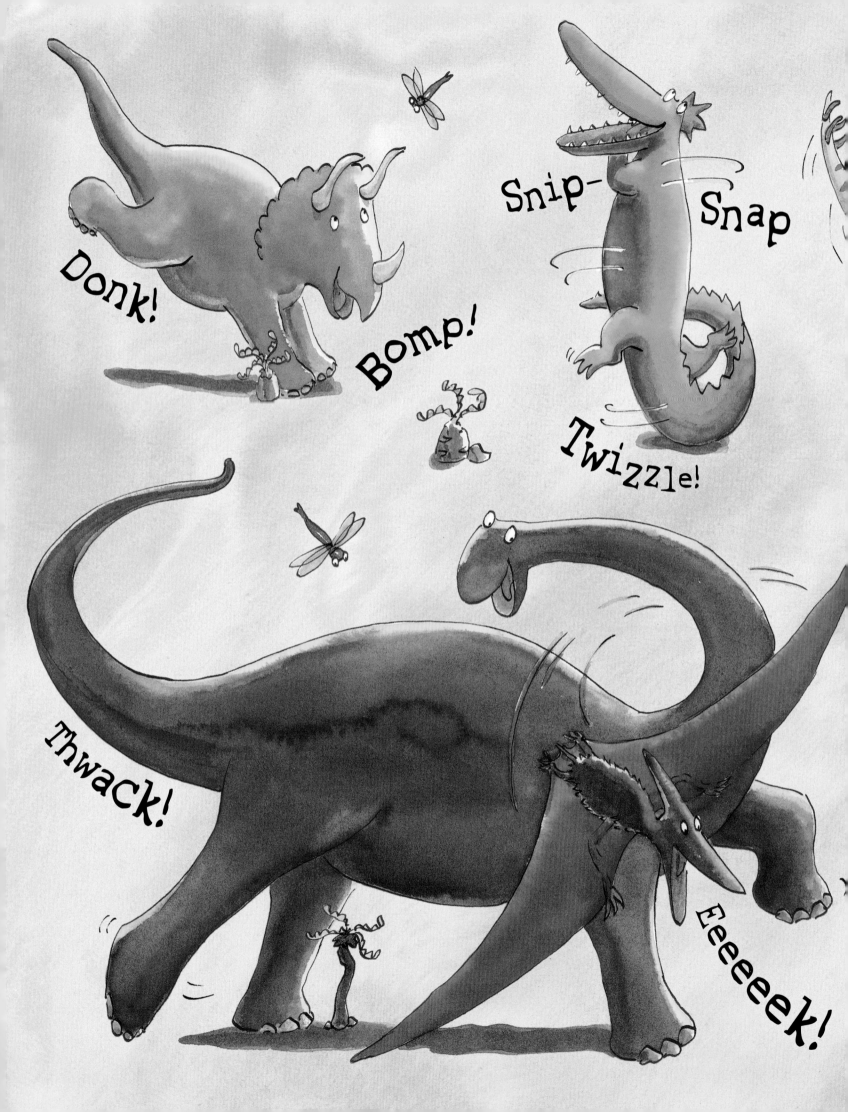

Clatter!

Rattle!

Zoom! Zoom!

Come and take a peek...

"Shake, shake, shudder...
near the sludgy old swamp.
Everybody's doing the
dinosaur romp.

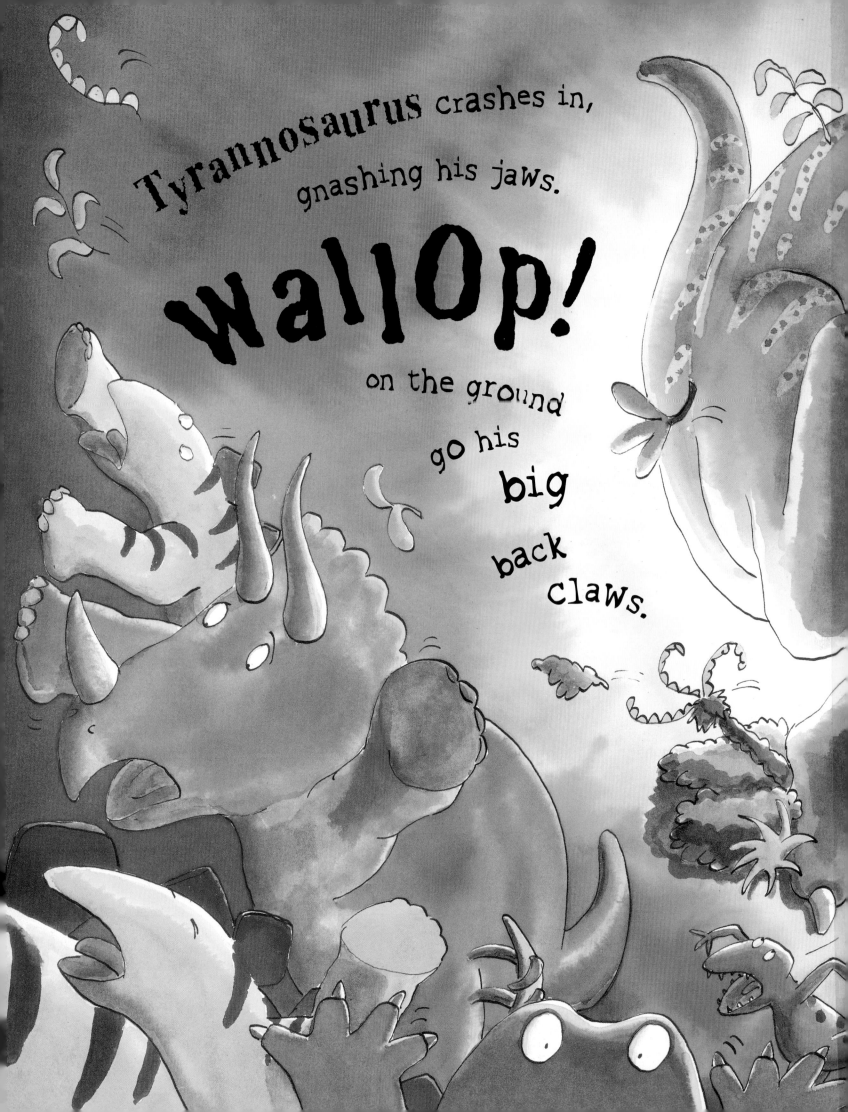

Tyrannosaurus crashes in,
gnashing his jaws.
Wallop!
on the ground
go his
big
back
claws.

He's huge
and he's heavy,
but all he wants to do...

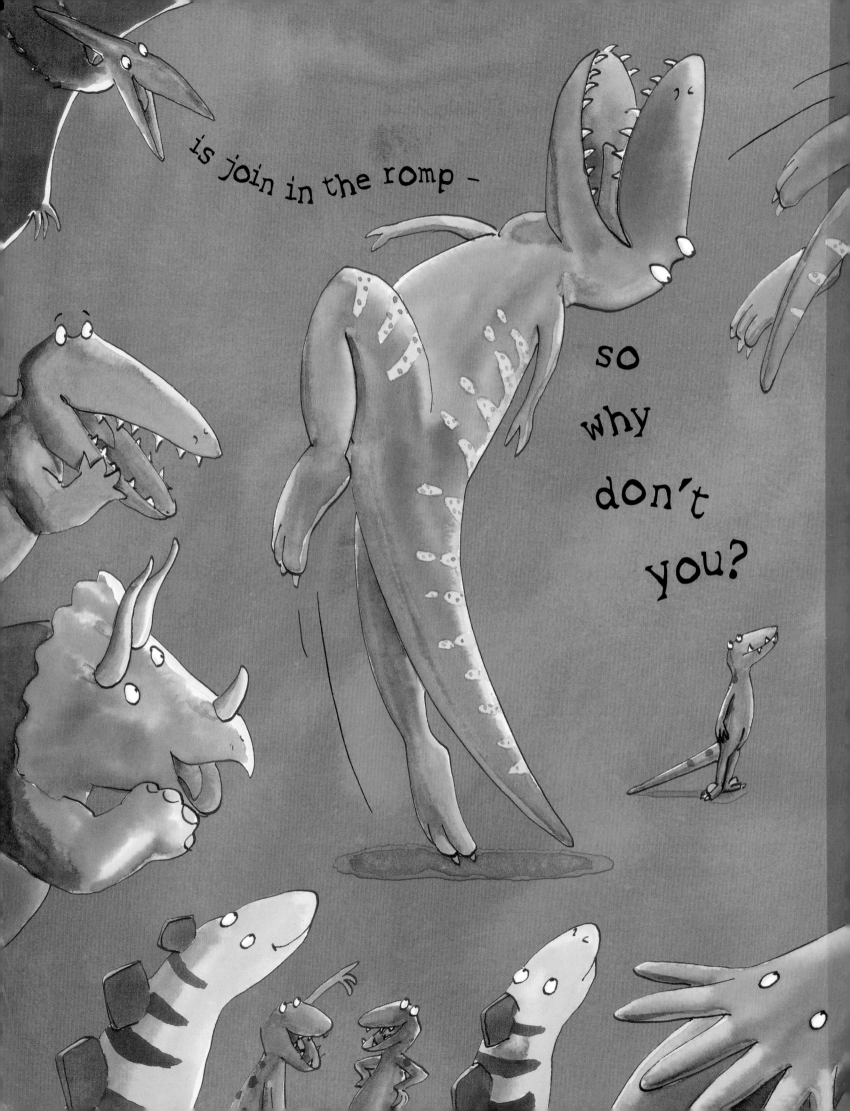

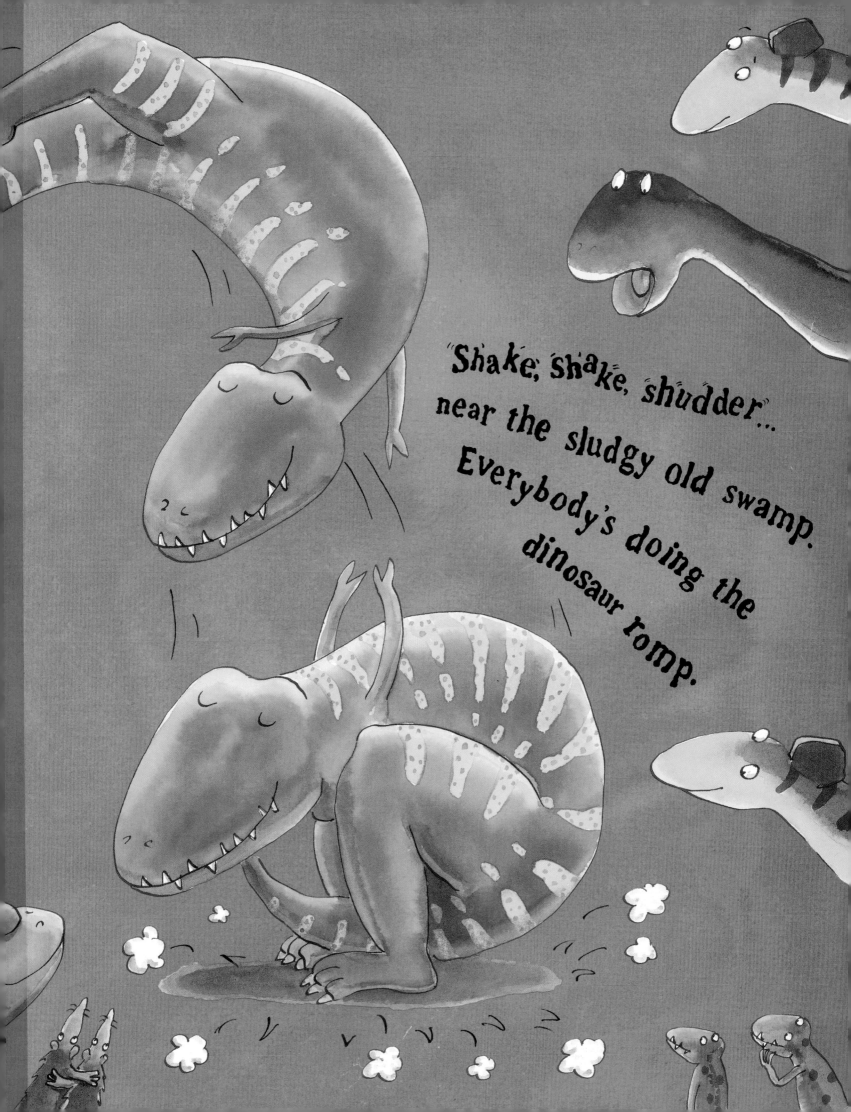

"Shake, shake, shudder...
near the sludgy old swamp.
Everybody's doing the
dinosaur romp.

The dinosaurs won't scratch us,
or bite us, or thump us.
They just want to holler up a...

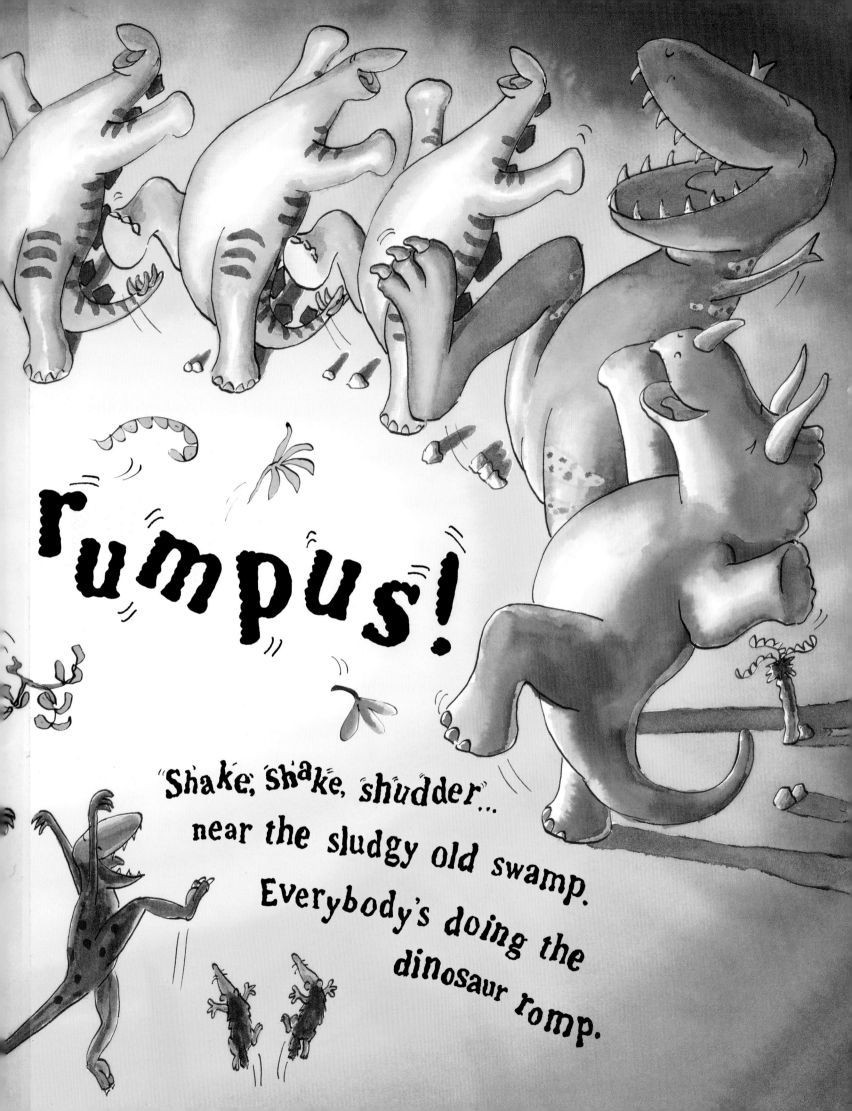

rumpus!

"Shake, shake, shudder...
near the sludgy old swamp.
Everybody's doing the
dinosaur romp.

But soon all the rompers grow sleepy and slow.

The rumpus calms down and the sound drops low.

The rompers drift together
and tumble in a heap...

till finally the dinosaurs
are all fast asleep.

And now the only noise
in the deep of the night
is...

dinosaur-snoring
till the next day's light.